Going Batty!

Going Batty!
L'épouvantable nuit d'Agatha Chauve-souris © 2004, 2005 Mijade Editions—Belgium
Text © 2004, 2005 Sylvie Auzary-Luton
Illustration © 2004, 2005 Marjolein Pottie

A publication of
Milk and Cookies Press, a division of ibooks, inc.

Distributed by Publishers Group West
1700 Fourth Street, Berkeley, CA 94710

This book is a work of fiction.
Any resemblance to actual events or locales or persons, living or dead, is entirely coincidental.

ibooks, inc.
24 West 25th Street, 11th floor, New York, NY 10010

The ibooks, inc. World Wide Web Site address is:
http://www.ibooks.net

ISBN: 1-59687-186-5
First ibooks, inc. printing: September 2005
10 9 8 7 6 5 4 3 2 1

Editor - Dinah Dunn
Associate Editor - Robin Bader

Designed by j.vita

Library of Congress Cataloging-in-Publication Data available

Manufactured in China

Going Batty!

by Sylvie Auzary-Luton

illustrated by Marjolein Pottie

MILK &
COOKIES
PRESS

Distributed by Publishers Group West

Bertha Bat lives with
her family in a cave,
deep in the forest.

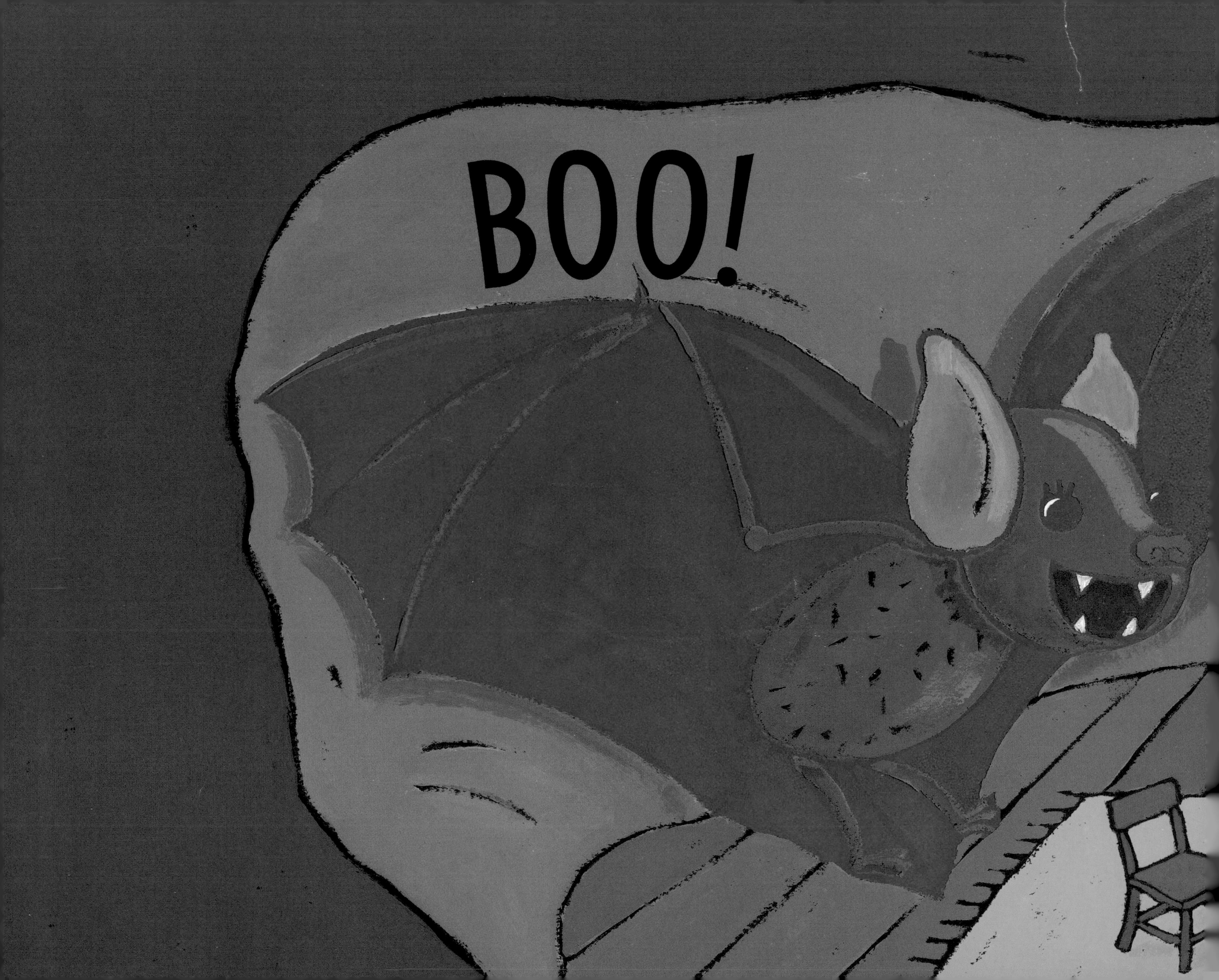
BOO!

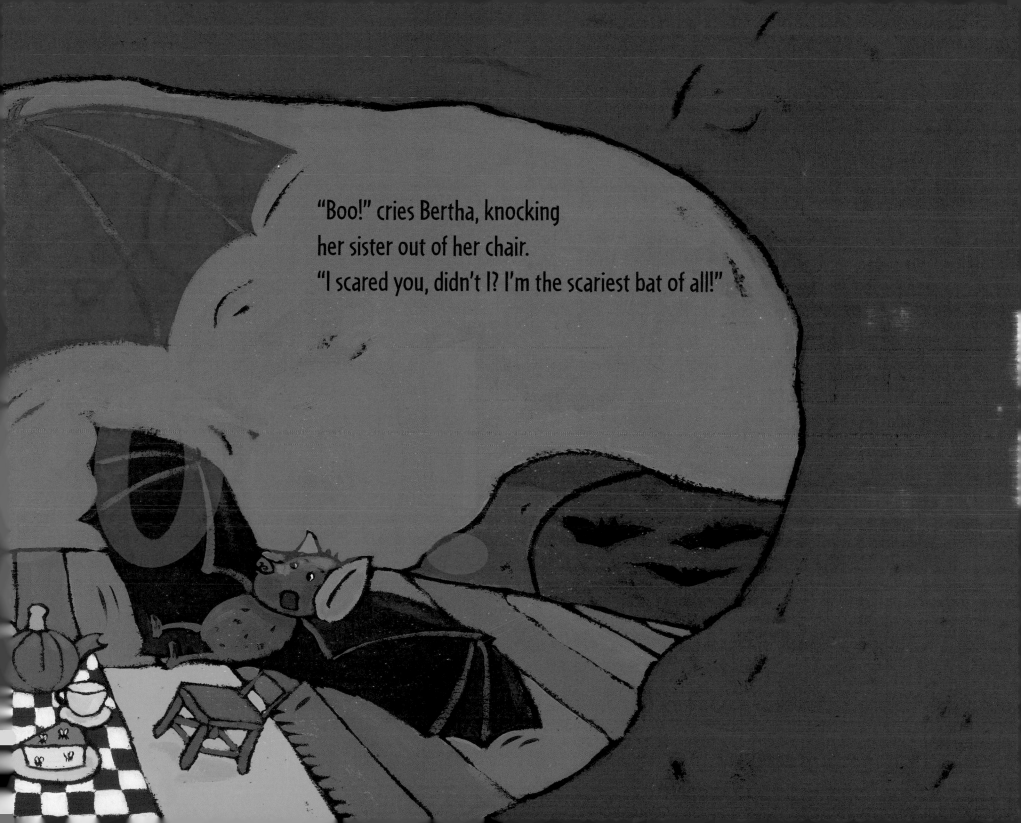

"Boo!" cries Bertha, knocking
her sister out of her chair.
"I scared you, didn't I? I'm the scariest bat of all!"

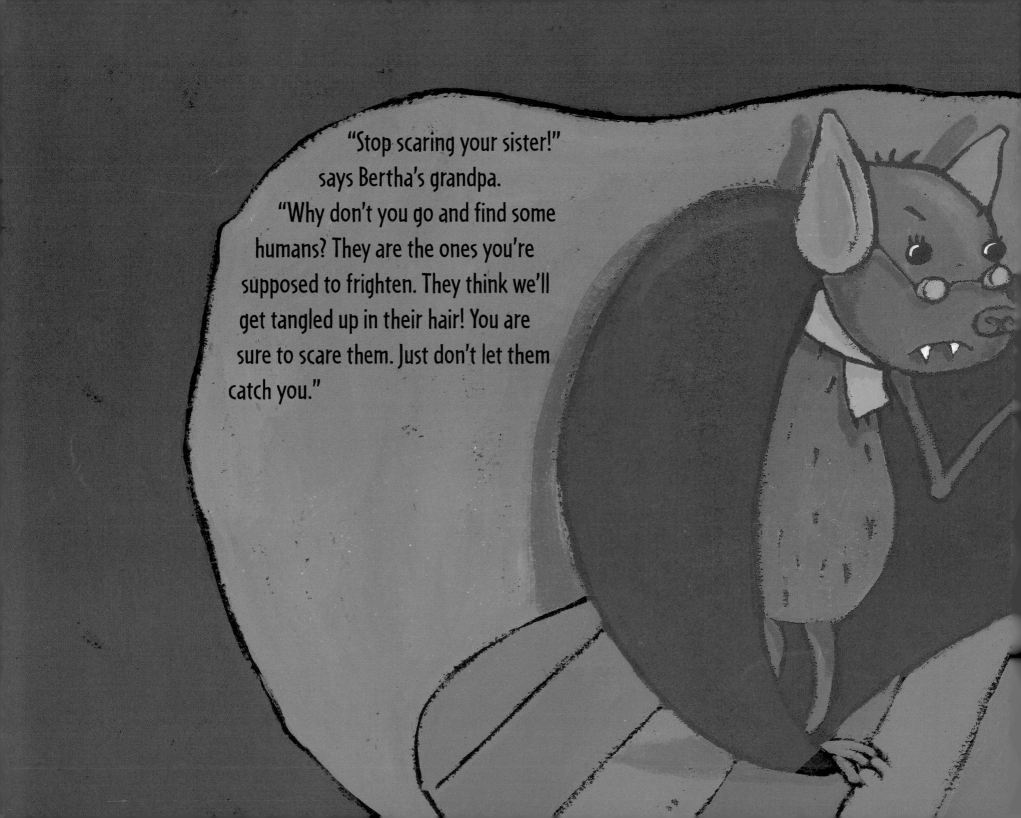

"Stop scaring your sister!"
says Bertha's grandpa.
"Why don't you go and find some
humans? They are the ones you're
supposed to frighten. They think we'll
get tangled up in their hair! You are
sure to scare them. Just don't let them
catch you."

Bertha goes into the bathroom to get ready.
"I'm going to be Queen of the Night!" she says.
She sharpens her claws to points like needles.

She combs her hair
straight up from her head.

She rubs her wings until they
shine in the moonlight.

"BOO!" she laughs into the mirror,
showing her sharp teeth.
"Ready or not, here I come!"

Bertha flies up to the village, ready to scare the first human she meets.

"I'm in luck," Bertha says to herself as she flies over the main square and spies a large crowd of people.

"There seems to be some kind of parade."

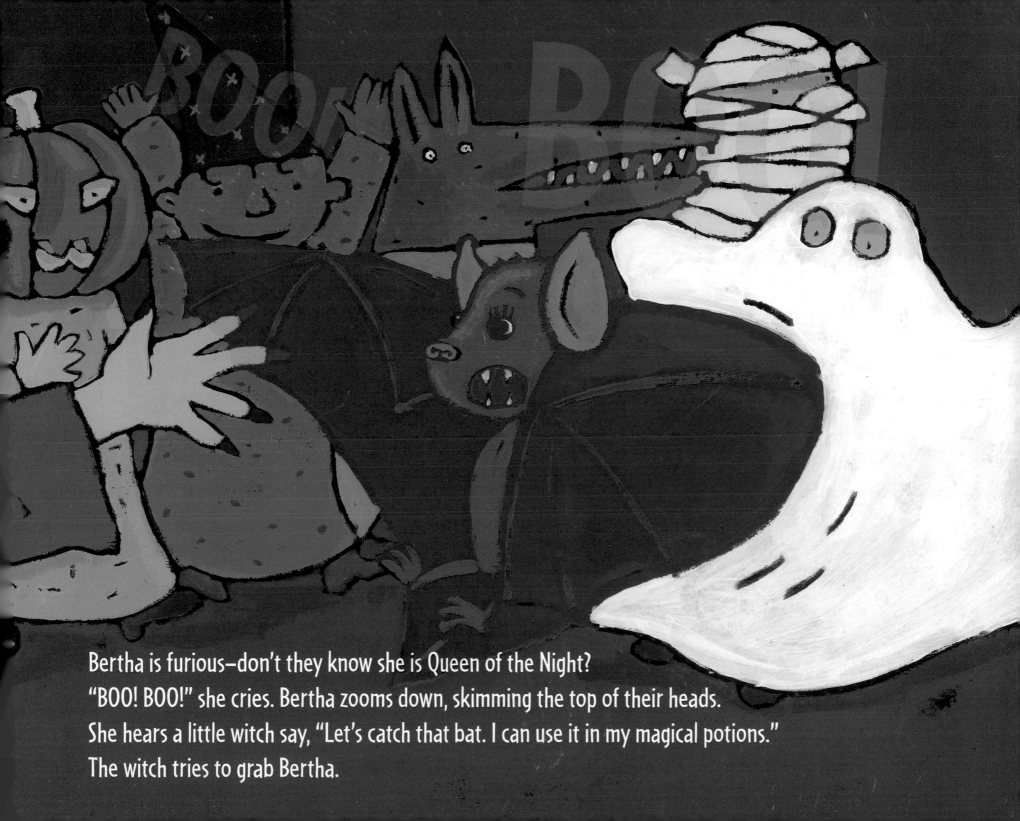

Bertha is furious—don't they know she is Queen of the Night?

"BOO! BOO!" she cries. Bertha zooms down, skimming the top of their heads.

She hears a little witch say, "Let's catch that bat. I can use it in my magical potions."

The witch tries to grab Bertha.

Bertha flaps her wings to get away, but she flies right into a ghost.

She turns to see the sharp fangs of a vampire and the witch's purple claws.

"I'm scared!" squeaks Bertha.

In her panic to get away, Bertha flies right into a skeleton!

"OH NO!" cries Bertha. "OH HELP! A skeleton!"

The skeleton laughs. "I'm not a real skeleton, silly! On Halloween, everyone dresses up in a costume to scare each other—that's what makes it fun. What would you like to be?"

Soon Bertha is flying over the crowd
again shouting:
"BOO! BOO! BOO!"
The people below clap their hands and
shout with delight.
"That is the best costume of all!"

When Bertha flies into her cave her whole family lets out a scream.
"BOO!" she cries, laughing with delight.

Bertha takes off her pumpkin mask.
"It's me!" she says. "I'm the Queen of the Night!"
"Bertha!" squeals Bertha's sister.
"Bertha!" shouts Bertha's grandpa.
"Bertha!" sighs Bertha's mother. "Thank goodness it's only you! Come along, it's time for bed."

As Bertha drifts off to sleep, she thinks,
"Next year I'll have to bring my whole family to the Halloween parade.
Now THAT'S scary!"

The End